PUMPKIN BUTTES

A Mary MacIntosh novel

Maureen Anne Meehan

PUMPKIN BUTTES

www. maureenmeehanbooks.com

info@maureenmeehan.com

Pumpkin Buttes Dedication

Pumpkin Buttes is dedicated to Paula Sue (Todd) Robertson, my dear friend from Buffalo, Wyoming, who reminded me this summer about the uranium in the Pumpkin Buttes. Paula and I were on the high school swim team together, attended the University of Wyoming where she and my other roommates were cheerleaders, and we have been best friends for over 40 years. Included with this group remain Sherry (Roach) Naddour, Kari Sue (Hill) LaHaye, and Debi (Marquardt) Baiel.

In addition, this novel is dedicated to family, friends, and loyal readers. Your continued support is greatly appreciated.

PUMPKIN BUTTES AUTHOR'S NOTE

May the road rise up to meet you, May the wind always be at your back, May the sun shine warm upon your face, the rains fall soft upon your fields, and until we meet again, may God hold you in the palm of His hand.

May God be with you and bless you. May you see your children's children. May you be poor in misfortune, Rich in blessings.

May you know nothing but happiness from this day forward.

May the road rise to meet you. May the wind be always at your back. May the warm rays of sun fall upon your home and may the hand of a friend always be near.

May green be the grass you walk on. May blue be the skies above you. May pure the joys that surround you.

May true be the hearts that love you. May God be with you and bless you.

May you see your children's children.

May you be poor in misfortune, rich in blessings. May you know nothing but happiness.

From this day forward.

Table of Contents

Chapter 1

Native Americans have always played a crucial role in America and their presence in the West remains strong. During Wyoming's frontier era, the Pumpkin Buttes were used as Indian lookouts to monitor game, emigrants on the Lewis and Clark and Bozeman Trail, soldiers, and as tribal ceremonial locations. They served also as a convenient hideout much like that of the likes of Butch Cassidy and the Sundance Kid at the Hole in the Wall a few miles away from Pumpkin Buttes.

This area is geologically unique. It is not only beautiful, but it is organically rich. Uranium rich. It is also rich in high-tech alloys such as neodymium, praseodymium, and scandium, making mining in this area highly competitive and desirable to those who have access.

Uranium is a chemical element with a symbol of U and an atomic number of 92 and it is a silvery-grey metal in the actinide series of the period table. A uranium atom has 92 protons and 92 electrons, of which six are valence making its radioactive decay an alpha particle. The half-life of this decay varies between 160,000 and 4.5 billion years for different isotopes, making it useful for dating Earth's age. It's also useful for the atomic bomb.

The most common isotope in natural uranium is 238 making this the highest atomic weight and denser than lead.

The Pumpkin Buttes rise from rolling grasslands that surround the Powder River Basin and consist of three buttes. They are called the North Butte, the South Butte, and the Middle Butte. The names are not very original, but natives were much better known for their descriptions and their names were original and unique. Native Americans, mostly the Dakotas, referred to them as "Wohanble Thianca" which translates loosely to "Vision Quest Buttes." The buttes were considered sacred and were often used for spiritual rituals and vision quests. Natives would climb them for solitude, fasting, and prayer, seeking visions and guidance from the spiritual world.

The lands were fought over for decades commencing in the 1870s after the Indian Wars ended. Erosional remnants of topographic sediments preserved in the area originated from the roll front model of uranium deposition. In addition to uranium, there remain vast coal beds, oil, gas, and specifically methane gas that now powers the United States.

What seems to frustrate the oil and gas industry is the lack of access to this region as it exists on private land belonging to ranchers and the BLM. One must pay to play.

It is landlocked to private or public land.

If the greedy can't afford to pay, they cheat.

Chapter 2

The Hoskinson family owns a large ranch in Wyoming that contains rare minerals, and the family may or may not be connected to Cardano, a major blockchain platform. While specific details about the ranch and rare minerals aren't widely available, reports are suggesting that Charles Hoskinson has been involved in ventures connected to Wyoming due to the state's blockchain-friendly regulations.

Wyoming is also well-known for its natural resources and mineral wealth, and this ties nicely into potential mining activities or ventures involving rare minerals, but no specific details about the Hoskinson family being involved in the mineral extraction of these rare minerals are widely publicized.

These rare minerals are neodymium, praseodymium, and scandium, which are essential for high technology including cell phones and items of much higher worth. These three minerals are found on the Charles Hoskinson ranch and may or may not be extracted as part of the Malleck Creek project.

Chapter 3

Cameco Corporation is a Canada-based organization with significant operations in Wyoming. Cameco owns the Smith Ranch-Highland and North Butte uranium mines in Wyoming. It remains one of the largest uranium producers globally and exports uranium to various countries for use in nuclear power plants. In conjunction with agreements with the governments of the United States and purchasing countries, together they try to ensure that the material is used for peaceful purposes, in line with international agreements. The process is overseen through agencies such as the Nuclear Regulatory Commission and the Department of Energy.

Uranium production in Wyoming happens primarily through in-situ recovery (ISR) mining, which is considered an environmentally friendly and cost-effective method of extracting uranium. Key uranium mining regions in Wyoming include the Powder River Basin and the Wind River Basin.

The export process involves nuclear fuel supplies and intermediaries who purchase the raw material. The uranium is usually processed and enriched before it is shipped abroad. Exports are highly regulated to ensure compliance with international nuclear agreements and non-proliferation protocols.

In addition to Cameco, Ur0Energy operates the Lost Creek ISR uranium facility in south-central Wyoming. Ur-Energy produces and sells uranium for both domestic and international markets, including export through nuclear fuel brokers.

Uranium was discovered at Pumpkin Buttes in 1951. The ore bodies are within and adjacent to red-stained channeled sandstones at redox roll fronts in the Wasatch Formation of Pumpkin Buttes. Originally the only uranium market was with the U.S. Federal Government which used uranium in Cold War armaments. The first commercial nuclear power plant in the United States was opened in 1958. Wyoming operators have used only the ISR mining technique since 1993.

Since Three Mile Island in 1979, Chernobyl in 1986, and Fukushima Daiichi in 2011, there has been increasing resistance to nuclear power generation. Currently, there are 58 commercially operated nuclear power plants with 96 nuclear reactors in 29 U.S. states, and the majority of these are located east of the Mississippi River.

In 2015, five ISR projects were operating in the Powder River Basin, with several additional in the permitting and planning states. However, today there are only a few sites that remain active in this area of Wyoming. The Nicholas Ranch and the Lance ISR projects are the largest.

Pumpkin Buttes has long been part of the play in the oil and gas industry of Wyoming. The first petroleum boom in the Powder River Basin began with the discovery of Salt Creek field 34 miles southwest of Pumpkin Buttes along the Casper Arch in 1908. The first commercial oil discovery in the Pumpkin Buttes area was the Pennsylvania Minnelusa oil reservoir in 1948 at Adon Field north of Gillette. Conventional reservoirs in the area range from Mississippian to Paleocene. Wyoming holds three percent of the nation's proven crude oil reserve.

Unconventional coal bed methane plays began in the 1990's in the Tertiary coals with the drilling boom lasting from approximately 1998 to 2008.

Fracking was the preferred method for coal bed methane extraction, but it comes with a high price to the environment. A perfect example of this was Buck Branaman's ranch outside of Sheridan Wyoming. Buck Branaman and his wife, Mary, are the famous "horse whisperers" and the subject of novels and movies. They are down-to-earth hard-working people. When the mineral rights were bought out from under their ranch during this timeframe, the fracking to extract the coal bed methane beneath their ranch destroyed their horse training business and ultimately their ranch.

Wyoming was the third largest coal bed methane producer in the nation. The majority of the wells have since been plugged due to the depletion of low natural gas prices.

In 2010 and beyond, the industry began to focus on horizontal drilling and fracking oil and gas Cretaceous sandstones of the Teapot, Parkman, Sussex, Shannon, and Frontier/Turner and source rocks of the Niobrara and Mowry Formations.

Chapter 4

The name Alcatraz is derived from the Spanish "Alcatraces." In 1775, the Spanish explorer Juan de Ayala was the first to sail into what is now known as the San Francisco Bay and he knew that the area was unique. The exact meaning of the name of the island is debated, it is universally agreed that the meaning can be defined as "pelican" or "strange bird."

In 1850, a presidential order set aside the island for use as a military post, and during the California Gold Rush, the boom of the Bay Area and the need to protect the bay led to the U.S. Army building a fortress at the top of the island. The Army also made plans to install cannons around this citadel, making Alcatraz the most heavily fortified military outpost of the West.

Alcatraz is one of three islands and its neighbors, Fort Point and Lime Point, formed a triangle of defense for the Bay. By the late 1850's, prisoners were housed on the island and its role as a prison morphed from a military base.

In 1909, the Army tore down the Citadel, leaving its basement level to serve as the foundation for a new military prison which matriculated to be known as "The Rock."

The U.S. Army used the island for more than 80 years and then was transferred to the U.S. Department of Justice for use by the Federal Bureau of Prisons.

Based on location, the Federal Government decided to open a maximum-security, minimum-privilege penitentiary to deal with the most incorrigible and dangerous inmates and it was known as a resting point for some of the worst criminals in the 1920's and 1930's. For example, Al Capone, George "Machine-Gun" Kelly, Alvin Karpis ("Public Enemy #1"), and Arthur "Doc" Barker served time on Alcatraz as these were well-known gangsters of the era. This was where dangerous escape artists were housed.

Alcatraz was known for its strict enforcement of no frivolities, and the prisons had only four rights: food, clothing, shelter, and medical care. Any privilege had to be earned.

One of the most infamous prisoners was the "Birdman of Alcatraz," and Robert Stroud served for manslaughter on the outside before attacking another inmate at the prison he was originally sent to and then murdering a guard in prison in Leavenworth, Kansas. After the attacks, he was sent to Alcatraz. He never had any birds at Alcatraz but in Leavenworth, he did develop an interest in birds and eventually crafted two novels while serving about canaries and their diseases.

But the most famous prisoners from Alcatraz are the three men who escaped from the island prison in 1962. The escape attempt was clearly not the first, as there were numerous other failed attempts dating from 1936 through 1958. However, on June 11, 1962, three men vanished from their cells and were never seen again.

Frank Morris and brothers John and Clarence Anglin vanished from their cells in the middle of the night.

There was a fourth man, Allen West, who was widely believed to be the mastermind behind the escape, but he was still in his cell the morning after the escape.

It has long been a mystery as to what happened to Morris and the Anglin brothers. Some believe that they froze in the chilly waters in the San Francisco Bay. Some believe they were eaten by Great White sharks. Some believe that they were not strong swimmers and when their makeshift floating devices failed, they drowned. However, there is a large majority of fans who are fascinated by true crime and prison breaks, believe that these three men were successful in their plan and have never been seen or heard from again.

Chapter 5

The illegal export of uranium is nothing new and it has been going on for decades. Uranium is essentially stolen from areas like Pumpkin Buttes trucked through South Dakota, North Dakota, Canada, and Alaska, and eventually put on a ship that sails the Bering Strait to Russia. In addition to uranium, there are foreign nationals who violate export controls by selling equipment to Russia's nuclear energy industry.

In fact, two men were charged with illegal smuggling and conspiring to violate export controls by selling such equipment to Russia quite recently. San Bhambhani of North Attleboro, Massachusetts, and Maxim Teslenko of Moscow were each indicted on one count of smuggling and one count of conspiracy to violate and evade export controls. These types of cases are quite common, yet shocking. Bhambhani and Teslenko conspired to export laser welding machines to the Ural Electromechanical Plant, or UEMZ, in Yekaterinburg, Russia. They falsified documents to conceal the fact that the equipment was going to UEMZ, which is a subsidiary of Rosatom, a Russian state corporation that oversees the country's civilian and military nuclear program.

Not only is there an ongoing probe into the Russian government's illegal export of machinery and uranium, but China is also the subject of such a probe, which won't surprise most readers.

The U.S. government is investigating China for importing and using Russia's uranium in its own power plants, and then exporting domestically produced uranium to the United States, thus undermining the U.S. ban that is intended to deprive Moscow of revenue for its invasion of Ukraine. This activity is banned by the U.S., which blocks imports from Russia and is part of massive sanctions on Moscow over its war on Ukraine. This boost in enriched uranium shipments from China and the potential circumvention of the ban has also raised concern in the U.S. that the uranium fuel supply chain industry will continue to be undermined by such activity.

Chapter 6

Native Americans occupied Alcatraz Island from November 1969 to June 1971 as part of a protest movement to highlight the issues of Native American rights, sovereignty, and mistreatment by the U.S. government. After Alcatraz Prison was closed in 1963, a group of Native American activists, led by Richard Oakes and the group "India's of All Tribes" or IAT, claimed the island based on the 1868 Treaty of Fort Laramie. The treaty stated that all retired, abandoned, or out-of-use federal land would be returned to Native Americans.

The occupation sought to raise awareness about broken treaties, poor living conditions on reservations, and the loss of Native lands. The protest also called for the creation of a cultural center and a Native American university on the island. Though the occupation eventually ended in 1971, it became a significant moment in the Native American civil rights movement, inspiring future activism and contributing to changes in U.S. policy towards Native peoples.

The Fort Laramie Treaty of 1868 was signed by the United States government and the Oglala, Miniconjou, and Brule bands of Lakota people, Yanktonai Dakota, and Arapaho Nation. The treaty's goals were to establish peace between the tribes and white settlers and to relocate the tribes to the Black Hills in the Dakota Territory. The treaty guaranteed the Sioux the right to hunt in certain areas outside of the reservation. However, in 1876, a commission presented an agreement to the Sioux that was signed by only 10% of the adult male Sioux population. This agreement essentially broke the Fort Laramie Treaty of 1868.

The protest from the IAT on Alcatraz Island rebirthed the controversy regarding the Fort Laramie Treaty of 1868 and the subsequent multiple breaches of this Treaty. The Fort Laramie Treaty contractually obligated the U.S. government to return all retired, abandoned, or out-of-use federal land to the Indigenous peoples who once occupied it. As Alcatraz Prison had been closed on March 21, 1963, after the great escape of three men from the penitentiary, and the island had been declared surplus federal property in 1964, a number of Red Power activists felt that the island qualified for reclamation by Native Americans.

The protest and occupation of Alcatraz established a precedent for Indian activism. When Richard Oakes was shot to death in 1972, his death had a profound impact on the Native American Rights movement. Oakes had been a charismatic leader and advocate for Native issues. His death was a slap in the face to many within the movement. The man who shot him was a YMCA camp manager and claimed that it was in self-defense, and he was ultimately acquitted on the murder charge which sparked outrage among Native people. It further highlighted the injustices faced by Native Americans and it was motivational to those within the movement to continue to fight the fight for justice for Natives. His death was pivotal, and it is no coincidence that the Bureau of Indian Affairs in 1972 and the Wounded Knee standoff in 1973 were part of Oakes' legacy.

Chapter 7

One of the escapees from Alcatraz was Frank Lee Morris and it is important to note that he was orphaned at age 11 and was convicted of his first crime by the age of 13. Morris had spent most of his life in and out of correctional facilities. He was considered highly intelligent with a long rap sheet of crimes ranging from drug possession to armed robbery, and prison breaks. He served time at the Rock in January 1960 after a prison break from Louisiana State Penitentiary. He no sooner arrived at Alcatraz to begin planning his next escape.

He was introduced to John and Clarance Anglin soon upon arrival as they were well-known convicted bank-robbing brothers. In addition, he met Allen West who had been serving time at Alcatraz since 1957. They all knew each other from prior incarcerations at various prisons around the country, and within no time at Alcatraz, they were housed near one another and sat up late into the night speaking with each other from cell to cell.

It is agreed that Morris and West were the brains of the bunch, and the four began concocting an elaborate plan of escape. West had been serving time there for a long time and he knew the ins and outs of Alcatraz. His idea was to chisel away at the salt-damaged concrete around the air vents under their sinks in their respective cells. Using metal spoons stolen from the mess hall, a drill made from a vacuum-cleaner motor, and discarded saw blades, they dug through to an unguarded utility corridor.

Morris decided to mask the noise of this evening's drilling by playing his accordion during the hour set aside when music was played for the prisoners.

Once the whole was large enough to crawl through, they set up a makeshift workshop in the utility corridor. In this workshop, they used papier-mâché to create false vents to cover the holes. In this workshop, they constructed a rubber raft and life vests from stolen raincoats. They sealed the rubber "raft" by melting the plastic together using the hot water pipes inside the walls. They converted a concertina tool to inflate the raft and created paddles out of makeshift plywood that they absconded from the yard back into their cells.

So as to not miss nighttime cell checks, they again used the paper-mâché routine to create heads to place on their pillows and covered them in real hair taken from the floor of the prison barbershop.

On June 11, 1962, they put the plan into place after cell check and shimmied down an outside drainpipe with their raft and life vests. They inflated these items near the Pacific Ocean water's edge and sailed away into the darkness.

Their escape was not discovered until morning, and it was assumed that by this time, they had either drowned, froze, or made it to land.

Chapter 8

Mary MacIntosh had been a defense attorney in Jackson Hole and Sheridan, Wyoming for over 20 years, and an incident at her cabin involving a serial killer at her cabin years prior made her realign her life. She took a job as County Attorney in Sheridan and was now a prosecutor.

She was recently married to the local sheriff, and she was playing catch up after their honeymoon to Montana to ski the Big Sky and stay as a guest of the Yellowstone Club.

Sheriff Burgess "Burg" and Mac were new to marriage, but they were not new to law enforcement. Burg had been a deputy for over 40 years and Mac had been a lawyer over 30.

Burg was getting indoctrinated to a new post in Sheridan and he had his work cut out for him. Sheriff Kane, his predecessor, had no doctrine. The office was a mess, literally and figuratively, and Burg was a person who appreciated organization and order.

Burg was worried about his tidiness when moving in with Mac, but he quickly watched her unpack, categorize, and stash neatly. She was going to be a breath of fresh air.

Mac had been in her office for years and it was business as usual, but Burg had been left with a disorganized mess that only he could organize. He worked late into the evenings after their union and honeymoon, but this was not an impediment to their relationship. She had a new case pending that was unique and was giving her a twist in the law.

Chapter 9

In Wyoming, the regulation and export of uranium, like other nuclear materials, is governed by both state and federal laws. The key to these laws is first and foremost.

Wyoming assumed control over regulating uranium and other radioactive materials in 2018 through its Agreement State status with the U.S. Nuclear Regulatory Commission ("NRC"). This status allows Wyoming to regulate certain radioactive materials, including uranium, within its borders, which if one knows anything about the citizens of the state, would understand this negotiation. Wyoming is a "live and let live state."

The Wyoming Department of Quality oversees uranium mining, milling, and reclamation activities and some say that this is a joke. Some opine that the only thing this overpaid government office does is look the other way.

The Federal Regulations including the Atomic Energy Act of 1954 that governs the production, use, and disposal of nuclear materials have bite. This Act prohibits the unauthorized export of uranium, and it carries significant penalties for violations. The NRC also regulates the export of nuclear materials under the AEA and a license is required for any uranium export, and the NRC must approve any transfers out of the United States. This is laughable to many in Wyoming, as one must obtain a license to mine nuclear alloys, but one does not need a license to become a parent.

Chapter 10

Charles Hoskinson hired reliable people to work his ranch and three of these well-seasoned men were hired by his predecessors in the early 1970's and showed up every day with a "can-do" attitude that Hoskinson appreciated. He did not know everyone on the ranch, as it was a big operation, but he knew the key players. He managed cattle and sheep, and this was a big business, but he also bailed hay for other ranches and even tended to his tomatoes, zucchini, and pumpkins, which in the Fall were gigantic and sold at the Buffalo Farmer's Market on Saturday mornings in September and October each year.

His pumpkins were famously large and were a hot commodity near Halloween. At Octoberfest every October, there was a pumpkin-carving contest, and he was not only one of the judges, but he supplied the cash prizes for the top three winners. The caption on the ribbons that accompanied the cash prizes read, "Best Pumpkin from Pumpkin Buttes."

The Pumpkin Buttes are a series of prominent hills located in the Powder River Basin of northeastern Wyoming. These buttes stand out against the otherwise relatively flat landscape, with their striking orange-red coloration, which is reminiscent of pumpkins and gives them their name.

Geologically, the Pumpkin Buttes are made up of sandstone and shale, capped with hard sandstone layers that have resisted erosion. The area around them is rich in natural resources, including coal, oil, methane gas, and uranium, making it historically significant for mining activities.

The buttes are also notable for their archaeological importance, as artifacts from Native American cultures, including arrowheads and other tools, have been found in the area. In addition, woolly mammoth skeletons and dinosaur skeletons have been discovered in the area, including T-Rex, Stegosaurus, and Brontosaurus.

This region is sparsely populated, providing a remote and rugged feel, and is popular for outdoor activities such as hiking, biking, wildlife observing, fishing, and hunting. The views from the top of the buttes offer expansive vistas of the surrounding plains with wide-open skies typical of the Wyoming landscape. The entire state is scarcely populated, and there are more antelope in Wyoming than there are people. Wyomingites love this. They love the wildlife and expansive space, clean air, lack of traffic, and the fact that folks are kind friendly, and helpful with one another.

Charles Hoskinson loved this about the state. People were genuine and kind and for the most part, extremely honest and down-to-earth.

Chapter 11

Mac had not been compelled to form a grand jury for an indictment since she took office, as these were rare in Wyoming. However, she was forced to do so over pending charges against two men who allegedly illegally exported uranium to foreign nationals in Russia and China. She would need to partner with the federal government and the case would be filed in Wyoming's Federal Court. If the grand jury found grounds to file, she would caption a complaint listing the federal court, jurisdiction, and case number, as well as a brief background outlining the nature of the charges.

Her research informed her that the first paragraph of the complaint would read something to the effect of, "The defendants are charged with violations of federal laws regulating the export of uranium, a nuclear material subject to strict governmental controls."

The jurisdiction portion of the complaint would establish that the crime took place in Sheridan County, Wyoming.

The relevant laws and regulations would include violations of the Atomic Energy Act of 1954, the Export Control Reform Act (ERCA), the International Emergency Economic Powers Act (IEEPA), the Nuclear Regulatory Commission of the Department of Energy, and possibly other laws. Mac had not completed her research, but she was homing in on what to expect.

The factual description of the illegal activity might include the type and quantity of uranium involved, the manner in which it was illegally exported, such as falsified export licenses and smuggling, and the destination countries which was crucial as Russia and China were subject to U.S. sanctions, and the timeline of the illegal activities.

The charges, if the grand jury found them to be true, would include the illegal export of nuclear material, conspiracy to commit illegal export, false statements, and violations of the Atomic Energy Act and the Export Administration Regulations.

If applicable, the indictment could demand forfeiture of any profits or assets obtained from the illegal activity, as well as the uranium itself if still in possession.

Possible penalties for the crimes could include imprisonment, fines, and revocation of export licenses or future trading privileges, as well as the surrender of a U.S. passport.

Mac called Burg about this new development. He had testified before grand juries in the past and could offer her some insight as to what she should expect.

Chapter 12

Mac and Burg were settling in. He had been married twice before so it seemed easy for him.

Mac was a single gal, and the transition was astonishingly easy but not expected. She assumed the worst. She did not expect that this man could be so wonderful. sensitive, polite, clean, and respectful of her in every way.

When she asked about his experience with grand jury testimony over dinner at home, he patiently explained his experience and perspective, and he offered her sage advice as to how to proceed. He did not tell her what to do. He just explained how he visualized it happening, especially due to the nature of the alleged crimes.

This grand jury would be a novel concept in Wyoming as it would be a seminal case. He understood the importance of getting this right and his patience when answering questions was accepted with gratitude.

She knew that she could formulate the legal side of this equation, but the practical side was what had her scratching her head. Grand juries were not addressed in law school, and she had never been a part of this side of the system.

She knew that this was going to be a big case if the grand jury came back with the recommendation to issue the indictment.

She also knew that there were ongoing investigations in other counties within Wyoming and these investigations would likely also lead to other future indictments. Other lawyers would look to her for guidance.   It was the type of pressure that made her excel. Her fear of failure made her fearless.

There were rumors circulating that illegal activity was ongoing in the Pumpkin Buttes, more particularly on the lands belonging to Hoskinson and the production of Cameco Corporation near the Smith Ranch Highland area on the North Butte of Pumpkin Buttes.

Chapter 13

Neodymium, praseodymium, and scandium are rare earth elements that play essential roles in modern technology. Neodymium is a key component in the production of powerful neodymium magnets, used in various applications such as electron motors, hard disk drives, headphones, speakers, and wind turbine generators. It is also used in neodymium-doped lasers for industrial cutting, medical procedures, and laser pointers. These magnets are critical in electric and hybrid vehicles as well.

Praseodymium is used in combination with neodymium in high-strength permanent magnets. It is also used in the production of specialized glass, such as for welding goggles or camera lenses, because of its ability to filter out certain wavelengths of light.

Scandium is used in aerospace and sports equipment, especially in aluminum-scandium alloys to produce lightweight and strong maters such as bicycle frames, baseball bats, and aircraft components. It is also essential for metal halide lamps for high-intensity lighting applications such as stadiums and film production. Scandium is also used in solid oxide fuel cells to enhance conductivity.

These three elements are crucial for producing durable, efficient, and lightweight components in various high-tech industries.

Wyoming has significant potential for rare earth elements such as these three which can be found in the northeastern part of the state in the Bear Lodge Mountains and also in the southeastern portion of the state. Scattered throughout Wyoming are smaller, less-developed rare earth prospects. These include areas with mineralized deposits of carbonatites and alkaline igneous rocks, which can contain rare earth elements like neodymium, praseodymium, and scandium.

These elements are found in the Pumpkin Buttes and in a high quantity on the Charles Hoskinson ranch. They are currently farmed through the Malleck Creek Project and are sold to high-tech companies in the cellular device's arena, car manufacturers, and other companies competing in these high-tech fields.

These rare earth elements are expensive, both to extract from the earth and in the sale of the elements once extracted. They garner a good return on investment and the landowners who have discovered these elements have learned the incredible value of mining them.

In conjunction with uranium found in this same area of the Pumpkin Buttes, it goes without saying that this land is rare, unique, and hotly fought for due to the wealth the rare earth elements can provide.

Hoskinson's ranch not only contains these elements, but it is also a cattle and sheep ranch, and he had many folks who live and work there managing herds, tending to fixing fences, and overseeing the mining exercises, and he does not know them all by name. He would like to, but it's a big operation and he only has discussions with the higher-ups.

Therefore, he was completely unaware that for years, three men worked his ranch and were on his payroll, but he didn't know their personal histories. It would be a shocking discovery when he eventually learns that Frank Morris and John and Clarence Anglin had been hiding out in this remote area of Wyoming since their escape from Alcatraz in 1962.

Chapter 14

The Anglin brothers had passed away years prior to lung cancer and old age, but Frank Morris was a cantankerous old man at the age of approximately 92 years and he still worked the Hoskinson ranch like he was a young fella. He was hunched over and crippled and stiff when he awoke, but he was also incredibly wealthy from the illegal export of uranium. He'd been in cahoots with Russian conglomerates for decades, running an illegal export business from the Pumpkin Buttes without detection.

Others had been caught. Morris was a career criminal. He was never going back to prison.

Chapter 15

The export of uranium, like other nuclear materials, is heavily regulated due to its potential use in nuclear energy and weapons. In the United States, uranium export requires strict compliance with federal laws and international agreements.

The export of uranium is controlled by the Nuclear Regulatory Commission in the U.S. Exporters, and one must obtain an export license from the NRC, which is responsible for regulating nuclear materials and ensuring that exports are for peaceful purposes. The exports must comply with international treaties such as the Treaty on the Non-Proliferation of Nuclear Weapons and agreements like the U.S.–Russia Peaceful Nuclear Cooperation Agreement. These agreements ensure that nuclear materials are not used for weapons development.

Exporters must provide detailed information about the end-use of the uranium and the facilities where it will be used. The importing country must agree to the use for civilian purposes and allow inspections by international bodies like the International Atomic Energy Agency.

In addition to the NRC, other U.S. agencies such as the Department of Energy and the Department of State may also be involved in the approval process to ensure that the export aligns with U.S. foreign policy and national security interests.

Failure to comply with these regulations can result in severe penalties, including criminal charges. For example, a grand jury indictment leads to criminal charges.

Chapter 16

Mac had her grand jury sequestered to deliberate on the charges in Sheridan, County for the two men who were caught allegedly illegally exporting uranium from Wyoming to Russia. The twelve-member jury took only an hour to return with the recommendation to indict on all charges. It was a pretty obvious case.

Once she dismissed the grand jury, she was able to finalize the charges to be filed that same day in the courthouse that was above her office in downtown Sheridan.

The Sheridan County Courthouse is a historic building that embodies classical revival architecture. Built in 1901, it features a symmetrical design with grand columns, a prominent pediment, and a central clock tower that dominates the façade. The courthouse was constructed from locally sourced materials, including sandstone, which gives it a rustic yet stately appearance. Its interior houses courtrooms and county offices, and the building has been central to the community for over a century. It's listed on the National Register of Historic Places due to its architectural significance and role in local history.

When Mac was satisfied with the charging papers, she had her assistant walk them to the criminal case filing window. The filing of the paperwork was relatively standard fare. Finding these two guys would prove to be a challenge.

Chapter 17

Judge Maurita Redle was the consummate professional and even though this case would be a case of first impression in Wyoming, she educated herself on the illegal export of uranium charges and handled the arraignment with poise.

The two defendants were appointed the public defender and Mac knew that this woman would do the bare minimum on their behalf.   It made her prosecutorial job easier, but Mac didn't appreciate the fact that it could set the case up for an appeal based on the defense of ineffective counsel.

The two men had been found hiding out in South Dakota. The governor of South Dakota was a "baller", and she did not put up with any garbage from anyone. Kristi Noem was a Harley-riding badass and a very smart, talented, and effective leader.   She was born in Watertown, South Dakota, and coming from a small town, was friends with Sheridan dentist, Patrick Meehan, who was also born in Watertown. When Noem learned that these criminals were camped out near Rapid City, South Dakota, she sent the troops in to arrest and extradite these guys to Sheridan for arraignment.

Sheriff Burg drove to Rapid City to escort these men to Sheridan and ensure that there were no attempts to escape. He put them in separate jail cells at headquarters downtown and put them on a deputy one-to-one to make sure that there was no communication with them except to assist with their activities of daily living such as food and showers.

Burg would not speak with either of these men as it could be perceived as a conflict of interest in that he was married to Mac. They were well aware that their relationship carried with it some built-in complications when it came down to her prosecutorial duties, and they took this possibility very seriously.

Burg did not want to interfere with Mac's cases, and he knew that he would need to assign two other deputies to oversee these men. He built what is known in the law as a "Chinese firewall" to ensure that he had no communication with these criminals or the deputies who monitored them. He spoke to the deputies about their duties, but they were informed that they were not to communicate any conversations they had or overheard so that Burg could remain neutral in the prosecution of these crimes of first impression in Wyoming.

Chapter 18

In Wyoming, like other places, there is a growing interest in using robotic and automated systems, including "bots" for various purposes. These range from agriculture and energy to healthcare and customer service. Specifically, Wyoming has a significant agricultural sector, and bots are being used to automate various tasks, from planting and harvesting to monitoring soil health and livestock. Drones, which can be considered aerial bots, are used for surveys and crop monitoring.

With Wyoming's heavy involvement in energy production, both fossil fuels and renewable energy, bots are employed to monitor and maintain remote facilities, inspect pipelines, and perform other high-risk tasks. Automation is also used in mining operations, reducing the need for human labor in hazardous environments.

Frank Morris was no stranger to bots. When a prisoner at Alcatraz, he was so far ahead of the curve with innovation that other inmates looked to him for guidance with respect to ingenuity. If this man had ever turned his life around and used his brilliance for good measure, he would have been a trendsetter and likely at the helm of the Amazons and Microsoft of the world.

Bots and automated systems have been integral to uranium extraction, which has a significant history in Wyoming.

Wyoming is the largest producer of uranium in the United States, and much of the mining activity occurs through a method called in-situ recovery or "ISR", which is less invasive and more environmentally friendly compared to traditional mining.

In-situ recovery involves injecting a solution (usually water with dissolved oxygen and carbon dioxide) into underground uranium deposits. The solution dissolves the uranium, which is then pumped back to the surface for extraction. ISR is commonly used in Wyoming because of the geology of its uranium deposits.

In ISR, automation is crucial. Bots, including drones and remotely operated systems, are used for many purposes. Automated systems track the flow of the solution and monitor the pressure and conditions of injection and extraction wells.

Bots help monitor and adjust the chemical composition of the solution used to extract uranium, ensuring efficiency and safety. Automated bots can collect and process vast amounts of data in real time, improving the accuracy of the extraction process. Robots are used to inspect and maintain pipelines, pumps, and other infrastructure involved in the ISR process, especially in remote areas where human presence is limited.

The use of bots minimizes the need for humans to work in potentially hazardous environments, especially in areas with radiation. Automated systems help ensure the solution used in ISR does not contaminate surrounding groundwater, as precise monitoring and adjustments can be made in real time.

Wyoming's uranium mining industry continues to evolve, and the integration of bots and automation plays a vital role in making the process safer, more efficient, and more environmentally responsible.

Frank Morris thought of this as early as 1965 after his successful escape from Alcatraz.

Chapter 19

Frank Morris figured out how to automate the extraction of uranium by the late 1960s and put his ingenuity to work. Illegally, of course.

He was a ranch hand on the Charles Hoskinson ranch in the Pumpkin Buttes and worked silently among other ranch hands, in particular, his two fellow Alcatraz escapees. They knew not to draw attention to themselves and did exactly what they were told to do. Nothing more. Nothing less.

This allowed Frank Morris the time to figure out that there was uranium on the ranch long before it would be discovered and it also allowed him to put his criminal mind to work on how to extract it.

He borrowed a library card from a fellow worker and when they went to town to purchase ranch equipment, he snuck off to the local library and checked out books on rare earth elements and how one could extract them.

The rest is history.

Chapter 20

Mac spent the weekend preparing for her upcoming trial for the two criminal defendants accused of the illegal export of uranium from Wyoming to Russia.

She was rushing to get to the courtroom on time for her pre-trial conference before Judge Maurita Redle. There was no need to rush, however, because Judge Redle took the bench, Mac was present at the prosecutor's table and the two defendants were shackled and seated at the defense table, but the public defender, Rosemarie Rodifer was late, as usual.

"Ms. MacIntosh," Judge Redle said, "have you heard from Ms. Rodifer this morning?"

"No, your Honor, I have not, but that is not out of the ordinary. She rarely returns my calls unless she needs something," Mac retorted. Mac could not stand Rosemarie. She was lazy and a terrible attorney and Mac had no idea how this woman passed the Wyoming bar examination. She rarely showed up to court on time and when she waltzed in and graced the courtroom with her presence, she acted as though she was doing everyone a favor.

Suddenly the courtroom door swung open, and Rosemarie strutted to the defense table carrying nothing but a blank legal pad and wearing what appeared to be street clothes. She looked as if she had just rolled out of bed. Her hair was unkempt and greasy. One could detect a mild glare from the ever-so-stoic Judge Redle, who was always dressed to the nines.

"Nice of you to show up," Judge Redle snarked at Rosemarie. "You look as prepared as you normally are."

Mac was amused. This was slightly out of character for Judge Redle. She rarely showed her cards, and for the judge to exude sarcastic commentary on the bench was unheard of.

"My apologies," Rosemarie said bluntly and without intent. "My alarm did not go off this morning."

"You know what they say about excuses," Judge Redle continued, before getting down to the nuts and bolts of the pre-trial conference.

Chapter 21

Cameco Corporation, a major uranium producer based in Canada, operates uranium extraction facilities in Wyoming. The primary site is the Smith-Ranch-Highland operation, located near Casper, Wyoming. This facility is known for using in-situ recovery (ISR) technology to extract in a more environmentally friendly and less invasive method compared to traditional open-pit or underground mining.

The Smith-Ranch-Highland facility is one of the largest ISR operations in the United States and has been a significant contributor to the uranium market. This method involves circulating a solution underground to dissolve the uranium from the host rock and then pumping it to the surface for processing. Cameco also owns other properties in Wyoming, like the North Butte satellite facility in Pumpkin Buttes, which contributes to its production.

Cameco's Wyoming operations are important due to the state's rich uranium deposits and favorable regulatory environment for uranium mining. These projects are crucial in meeting the demand for uranium, primarily for nuclear power generation.

Frank Morris was well aware of Cameco, and he knew who the players were that legally extracted and sold uranium. He studied their process by sneaking into both the Smith-Ranch-Highland facility as well as the North Butte satellite facility mining operations. He watched and learned how to extract the uranium. He then created a robot to recreate this ISR extraction method and put it to use secretly, with the assistance of both Clarence and John Anglin, who joined him in Alcatraz with his escape plan.

Frank had always been a clever, self-taught man and could figure out just about anything if given the time, tools, and opportunity to do so. The entire escape plan was his ingenuity, and the Anglin brothers were lucky enough to be asked to join Morris in the escape. The Anglin brothers were not known to be very bright, but they were bright enough to listen to Morris and act upon his plan.

Morris was a career criminal, known for his high intelligence with an IQ reportedly above 130. He had been incarcerated in multiple prisons and was eventually transferred to Alcatraz in 1960 due to his repeated escape attempts elsewhere. Alcatraz, known for its strict security and isolation, was designed to prevent escapes, making this particular breakout legendary.

The three men worked secretly for months in the night, digging holes in their cells' walls. They rarely slept and relied heavily on the morning strong coffee available in the mess hall. The guards had absolutely no idea that they were out of bed and up all night digging. They did not leave a trace of cement, stucco, or drywall behind as clues.

The FBI believes that Morris and the Anglin brothers likely drowned in the cold, rough waters of the San Francisco Bay, and there was no definitive evidence of their fate. Over the years, there have been various reported sightings and rumors that they survived, but their exact whereabouts remained unknown. The case was closed by the FBI in 1979, but it continues to capture the public imagination, and some investigators still speculate that the escapees may have survived.

Survived they did. In a remote part of Wyoming. Not only did they survive, but they also thrived due to the illegal export of uranium. They were rich men.

Chapter 22

Mac went to trial on the two men charged with the illicit transport of highly controlled uranium across borders in violation of numerous national and international regulations. Charges included tightly controlled treaties like the Nuclear Non-Proliferation Treaty (NPT), as well as violations of national securities laws, breaches of international treaties, and various other criminal offenses such as smuggling, endangering public safety, and trafficking dangerous materials.

The public defender was her useless self during the trial, rarely objecting to any expert testimony. Mac had done her homework and her experts were solid. Governmental assets were at stake, and the U.S. government was quick to send Mac resources, including second and third-chair attorneys who had handled these types of cases in the past. They also supplied the experts and provided her with all previous trial transcripts and deposition transcripts that would assist her in formulating her prosecutorial strategy.

The jury came back unanimously and the sentencing before Judge Redle went as she expected. Both men received 20 years to life in prison and extraordinary penalties in the form of fines upwards of seven million dollars.

This was a case of first impression in Wyoming and would set Mac up as the expert in prosecuting Wyoming cases of illicit and illegal export of rare earth elements.

This would not be Mac's last case.

Chapter 23

"Howdy, partner," Charles Hoskinson said to the old man near one of his larger barns on the ranch.

"Hey," the old man said.

"I've seen you around for years. How long have you been working my ranch," Hoskinson continued.

"By the looks of me, probably too long," the old man joked. "I was hired in the 1960s."

"Oh Lord and you have stayed loyal all of these years, and this is the first time that we have spoken?" Hoskinson asked.

"You are a busy man, sir."

"Not too busy to meet the folks that make all of this possible. I feel terribly that we have not been introduced."

"Well, now we have." Frank Morris was worried that the owner would ask his name. He had always gone by the pseudonym of Larry Cook. He created a false birth certificate not long after his Alcatraz escape and it worked well enough to get him a few jobs along the way until he ended up at the Hoskinson ranch. When he was hired around 1965, there was no request for a social security card for employment, and since he had been grandfathered into payroll back in the day, no one had ever asked him for one, which was good. He couldn't provide one.

Ranch hands were paid cash every two weeks and Frank Morris had a bank account in Casper under the name of Larry Cook. He also had accounts in Gillette and Buffalo, as he was a rich man.

"You'll have to come to the house and have supper with me and the missus some evening soon," Hoskinson said.

"I'd be obliged."

Chapter 24

Burg had heard whisperings about another case being investigated regarding the illegal export of not only uranium but also rare earth elements only found in the Pumpkin Buttes that included neodymium, praseodymium, and scandium. He had his ear to the ground while having an aft-shift beer with the guys downtown at the Mint Bar in Sheridan.

A fellow officer said, "I heard that the feds are snooping around the Smith Ranch Highland and North Butte mine for more illegal activity."

"You don't say," Burg responded, "uranium again?"

"Uranium and other stuff that is for high tech," the officer said.

"You don't say," Burg repeated. "Is that the Cameco Corporation area or Hoskinson's ranch?"

"I can't say, but somewhere in Pumpkin Buttes."

"You would think that the export of such highly valued and dangerous alloys would be extremely tightly controlled," Burg said.

"You'd think."

Burg finished his beer and headed home to tell Mac.

Chapter 25

After neodymium, praseodymium, and scandium are extracted from the Earth, they undergo several processes to refine, purify, and prepare them for industrial use.

After mining, the raw material is usually in the form of an ore, which contains these elements mixed with other minerals and impurities. The first step is to crush and grind the ore to extract the valuable components. Methods like magnetic separation, flotation, and gravity separation are commonly used to isolate neodymium, praseodymium, and scandium from other minerals.

With respect to neodymium and praseodymium, both elements are part of the rare earth family and are usually found together in minerals like monazite and bastnasite. After physical separation, they undergo chemical processes like solvent extraction, where different solvents are used to selectively remove each element from a solution.

Scandium is often found in trace amounts, usually in ores containing other elements like uranium or thorium. It requires more complex chemical treatments like ion exchange and solvent extraction to isolate it from other elements.

Once separated, these elements are further purified to reach the desired purity levels required for industrial applications. This often involves several steps of reprocessing through chemical or physical methods to remove impurities.

Neodymium is most commonly used to produce neodymium magnets, the strongest type of permanent magnets available. These magnets are crucial in technologies such as electric vehicles, wind turbines, and hard drives. Neodymium is alloyed with iron and boron to create neodymium-iron-boron magnets.

Praseodymium is often used in alloys with other rare earth elements to create high-strength permanent magnets or in applications such as aircraft engines. It is also used in glass manufacturing to make welder's goggles and UV protection filters.

Scandium is alloyed with aluminum to produce high-strength, lightweight materials for aerospace, 3D printing, and sports equipment such as baseball bats and bike frames.

Beyond magnets, neodymium is used in lasers, ceramics, and glass coloration. Praseodymium is also used in ceramics, lighting, and as a catalyst in various chemical reactions. Scandium-aluminum alloys are used in aerospace components and solid oxide fuel cells due to their high strength and low weight.

The extraction and refining of these elements produce waste materials, including toxic chemicals and mining tailings. This waste needs to be treated and managed responsibly to reduce environmental damage. Some mining operations also focus on recycling rare earth materials to minimize waste.

Mining rare earth elements like neodymium and praseodymium, as well as scandium, has significant environmental impacts, including habitat destruction, water contamination, and radioactive waste in some cases.

As a result, there is ongoing research to develop cleaner extraction technologies, including more sustainable mining practices and improved recycling methods for rare earth elements.

Chapter 26

When Frank Morris arrived at Charles Hoskinson's ranch house, he was greeted by Hoskinson's wife. She opened the door invited him in and introduced herself.

"Pleasure to meet you," Frank said. "I'm mighty taken aback by this dinner invitation. I've lived near this ranch for over 50 years, and it is my first dinner invitation. Thank you, kindly."

"It is our pleasure to welcome you into our home and I apologize that this invitation was not extended your way years ago. Thank you for all of your help on the ranch over the years. Charles is most appreciative. He doesn't get to meet a lot of the ranch hands because they come and go quickly. He is astonished that you've been around this long, and he has not been introduced."

"I keep to myself, mostly. My cohorts both passed on about 15 years ago and I guess I'm too old for the youngens," Frank said. He handed her a bouquet of sunflowers as she closed the door behind him.

"Charles asked that I send you to his study for a highball before we meet in the dining room for supper," she said.

He followed her through the maze of this large wood and rock custom home and was in awe of the chandeliers and opulence of the woodwork tapestry and artwork.

Hoskinson had obviously been a big game hunter in Africa, as there were trophy heads of sable antelope, Thompson gazelle, cape buffalo, and the like mounted to the walls among taxidermy from the United States in the form of grizzly bear and elk. It was beyond anything that Morris had ever imagined.

Frank Morris was a very well-read man, but he was not well-traveled, as he could never hold a passport and was a convicted felon. He read of these places and saw pictures in National Geographic magazines of the like, but he had never been anywhere except the United States, and most of his travel was in custody in a sheriff's bus as he was transported from prison to prison. He could look out the window at the scenery across the United States, but he never experienced it in the wild.

He joined Charles Hoskinson in his private office, and they sat in front of a large stone fireplace in high-back leather chairs as the wife poured them each a whiskey high ball in Waterford crystal tumblers out of a matching decanter.

"So, tell me what jobs you have had on my ranch over these decades of work and dedication," Hoskinson inquired.

"Well, sir, I have done anything that has been asked of me. I've mended fences, built barns, fixed equipment, tended to cattle, sheep, and horses, cleaned stalls, bailed hay, drove the bailor, you name it," Morris responded.

"How did you learn how to do all of these things?"

"Watching, mostly. And listening. And following instructions. The bosses here have always been nice to us. And patient.

I wasn't used to that as a kid, and having it here is what has kept me grounded for decades. I like feeling useful and valued, and I have always felt that on your ranch."

"We have been lucky to have you, and please call me Charles."

"Thank you."

They chatted for another 30 minutes before they were summoned for supper.

As they approached the formal dining room, the pungent smell of garlic was the aroma that made his stomach growl. He had not had anyone cook him a home-cooked meal as an adult. Most of his adulthood was behind bars, and the prison food was terrible. He could not believe the feast that lay before him on this waxed and shining long wood table. Roast beef. Mashed potatoes. Green beans. Salad that was not from a sack.

"This looks and smells incredible," Frank said with earnestness and sincerity.

"We are happy to welcome you to our supper table. We wish we had extended this offer much sooner," Hoskinson said. "You must be around 90 years old. My dad, if living, would be around your age. But he was a smoker, and he died of lung cancer over 20 years ago."

"I'm sorry to learn of this," Frank said sincerely. "I never knew my dad really, and the two other ranch hands that I worked alongside on your ranch were smokers too and they both died years ago from lung cancer. A nasty way to go."

"It is terrible to watch someone you love gasping for air at the end.

My dad went into a death rattle that could be heard on the other end of the house. My wife had to leave for the night. She couldn't stand hearing him die."

"My pals were the same. We lived together in our home not too far from here and both of their deaths were just miserable to watch," Frank concurred.

"Well, let's toast to happier thoughts and we raise our glasses in honor of your service to this beautiful ranch."

"Cheers," Frank said, as he sipped his first glass of Bordeaux. It was delicious. He couldn't believe that he stuck to whiskey and beer after sipping on this lovely red wine from Italy.

Chapter 27

Frank Morris was growing nervous with what he perceived as feds snooping around Pumpkin Buttes. He'd recently learned about two men who had been charged, convicted, and sentenced to the illegal export of uranium from the United States to Russia, and he heard that the case went down in Sheridan, which wasn't too far from Pumpkin Buttes. He heard that the prosecuting attorney was a tough nut in court and that the judge didn't put up with any monkey business in court.

Morris was no stranger to courtrooms or prosecutors or judges, as he had been convicted of multiple felonies in his younger days before he was ultimately transferred to Alcatraz, affectionately referred to as the Rock. It got its nickname from the impossibility of escape. He proved them wrong in 1962 and had been living a life on the lam ever since and had avoided recapture by keeping his head down on the Hoskinson ranch. But now that there were rumors of the feds snooping around the area, he was nervous.

Frank Morris owned a small but nice ranch with the Anglin brothers just south of Pumpkin Buttes. They held the title in a blind trust and had all assumed false identification through false documentation that Frank created. He was a computer whiz early on and he had been gaming the system his entire life.

The ranch did not have cattle or sheep or sell hay. It was a non-operating ranch. Except that it was not.

It was fully operational in the sense that it could export illegal rare earth elements and had been doing so for decades without a hint of detection. Frank was a smart man. Smart criminals are a rare breed. Diamonds in the ruff, they say. He was wise, smart, intelligent, clever, and a sharp businessman. He negotiated all the deals. The Anglins were not allowed to participate in the business other than to perform their respective roles in the manufacturing process. They were to keep their heads down, mouths shut, and hands busy. This was the pact, and since they stuck to it, they had never been caught.

Morris was old, and he knew that his days were numbered. The concept of going back to prison did not sit well with him, but if he was charged and convicted of his side gig of exporting controlled minerals and alloys, he would die in prison.

He made a pact with himself that this would never happen. If caught, he would suicide by self-infliction or by cop. Either way, he was never going back.

Chapter 28

Mac received a notice from the feds that she would be appointed as the attorney for upcoming charges against another illegal uranium and other rare earth elements charges. The appointment was in writing from the White House, and it noted that she was appointed as temporary Wyoming Attorney General.

It turns out that the AG from Wyoming had passed away and the election for a replacement was in 2026 and there was room to grow for Mac. The nomination was swift due to her career in general and her recent wins, and therefore, she received the interim appointment.

Her first AG case would be Pumpkin Buttes and the illegal export of uranium and neodymium, praseodymium, and scandium. On the Pumpkin Buttes.

Chapter 29

Mac had never been understood men. She was not raised by a good one and she had the amazing opportunity to be hired by Harry and he taught everything. Literally. So, when it came to Burg, she simply took him at his word. She never questioned him. She assumed the truth. She assumed his love.

It would serve her well.

Chapter 30

When Frank Morris read in the Casper Tribune newspaper that Mary MacIntosh had been appointed interim Attorney General for the state of Wyoming, he knew that he needed to be concerned. The article mentioned that she was the prosecutor of the two men convicted of illegally exporting uranium to Russia and it mentioned her no-nonsense approach to cases.

The article also mentioned that she was recently married to Sheriff Burgess formerly the head of the force in Cheyenne. Morris knew of Burgess because when he was hiding out after his escape with the Anglin brothers, they camped about 30 minutes west of Cheyenne in a place called Vedauwoo, This recreational campground had large boulders and outcroppings and it was easy to disappear in this area that was otherwise desolate. Other "campers" in the area warned of Sheriff Burgess and his German Shepphard fleet and informed them that they best not stick to one place too long.

Frank was accepting of good advice for the first time in his life after the Alcatraz Island vacation, and he was always looking over his shoulder. He and the Anglins moseyed north from Vedauwoo and ended up in an area that was called Pumpkin Buttes.

Chapter 31

Charles Hoskinson was not pleased with being served with a search warrant for his entire ranch. In fact, the new Attorney General had requested a warrant for not only the Malleck Creek Project on his land but also the Smith Ranch Highland area and the North Butte Mine. Essentially, the warrant covered all land within the borders and boundaries of the Pumpkin Buttes.

Hoskinson and other landowners were served in mass that winter morning. The land was covered with frost as the temperatures had dipped to a breezy two degrees above zero. It was too cold to snow.

The livestock were huddled together in the pastures, and it was a miracle that these animals could survive such low temperatures, but they did.

Within the hour of service of the process of warrants, the feds emerged in force with ATVs and Suburbans and vans and helicopters. The entire area was abuzz with activity.

"What is going on, dear?" Hoskinson's wife asked, wearing a cozy robe, and slippers and holding a fresh cup of coffee.

"Feds. Search warrant. I have no idea. They are looking for folks who apparently have been illegally exporting uranium off the ranch," Hoskinson said.

"Were you aware of this?" she asked.

"Hell no. We don't do that, and you know that. I have never done an illegal thing in my life!" he retorted.

"Other than speed and text when you drive," she added.

He shot her a sideways glance. She knew that it was time to exit stage left. He was not amused, and she knew when to retreat.

Chapter 32

"Warrants were served this morning," Mac reported to Burg. They were seated at the island in their kitchen having breakfast.   It was early and it was cold outside.

"What do you expect to find?" Burg asked. He was in his navy robe, and she was in her white one. Her hair was a mess, and she had a dap of mascara under her eyes. He loved seeing her like this. It was his guilty pleasure to know that other humans did not get to witness her looking pure and innocent and adorably imperfectly perfect.

"I'm hoping that these people have been stupid," she said. Most criminals are.

Burg nodded in agreement. He watched her make her third cup of coffee, strong and black. He had no idea how she could stomach such sludge on an empty stomach. He loaded his with cream and sugar and needed his cereal with it to manage drinking the concoction that she made every morning.

"I'm learning that the best way to do what we think has been going on is to acquire the uranium from stockpiles that are poorly monitored. This can happen in larger outfits like the North Butte mine. Then they have to have connections to Russia. And they need to falsify documents of export. They create fake end-user certificates or alter shipping records. They would need to be on the black market, and they would need to transport on back country roads. They probably use small ports like in Canada somewhere."

"How did this come to the attention of the feds?" Burg asked.

"They were already looking into it during my trial against the two guys and it rose to the attention of the FBI, CIA, and the International Atomic Energy Agency," Mac said.

"Will you need to drive to Casper today?" Burg asked.

"Possibly."

"If so, can I drive you?"

Mac was amused. She was fiercely independent. She didn't respond right away, and Burg knew to withdraw. He also knew to never ever tell her to calm down if she was heated. It garnered the opposite reaction. He had learned that one the hard way.

Chapter 33

Frank Morris had never personally handled uranium. He and the Anglin brothers always snuck onto mining operations and "borrowed" already processed materials. The larger operations were closely monitored, but they also relied on humans to measure qualities and quantities, making it fairly ascertainable to skim.

That was the case until robotics were introduced. Once that happened, which was fairly recently in some of the Wyoming operations, Morris backed off. He did not want to risk getting caught.

Morris was aware, however, that there was no statute of limitations for the illegal export of uranium or other nuclear materials from the United States. This was because such actions were considered serious offenses, often categorized under national security, terrorism, and weapons proliferation laws. Crimes that threaten national security or involve nuclear materials fall under statutes that don't expire due to their potential long-term harm.

The Atomic Energy Act governs the handling, transfer, and export of nuclear materials. Violations can lead to severe criminal penalties, and Morris was well aware of severe criminal penalties.

Export Control Laws like the Arms Export Control Act or the International Emergency Economic Powers Act regulate the export of sensitive materials and technologies, including uranium.

18 U.S.C. Section 2332 governs the use of weapons of mass destruction which includes radioactive materials and has no statute of limitations.

18 U.S.C. Section 831 prohibits unlawful possession, use, or transfer of nuclear material, and has no statute of limitations.

Due to the gravity of offenses related to nuclear smuggling and their national security implications, prosecution can occur many years after the crime.

Frank Morris had been out of the business for two decades. The "bots" had made the decision easy for him. However, this did not mean he was scot-free.

Chapter 34

Mac was in their master bathroom blow-drying her long auburn hair. She wore light makeup, and she had already applied it and was putting the finishing touches on a few curls before heading to the office. Burg had the day off, and he couldn't resist sitting on the edge of the tub and watching her get ready for work. She couldn't hear a word he was saying and that suited her just fine. He was gabby in the morning. She was used to this being her quiet time.

Her routine was to go out for a run early while still dark, get home for her coffee, and then shower before work whilst reading the news online. She rarely heard a human voice until she reached the office. This all changed when Burg moved in. It was taking some getting used to. She was used to her three rescue kittens talking with her in their private conversations which others would find awkward. She was not used to the chatterbox that she married.

She assumed that Burg would repeat anything that she hadn't responded to if it was important. He rarely followed up, so she figured that he was filling the air with his voice in her bathroom for no other reason but to entertain himself.

"If you need to drive to Pumpkin Buttes today, please call me. I want to at least go with you," Burg pleaded.

He worried about her driving on icy highways and back country roads by herself. He secretly stashed blankets water and snacks and a flare gun in the back of her SUV.

"I'm good," was all that he received in reply.

He was used to her independence, and he adored her for her fierce identity, but he needed to be needed by her, and he knew that she didn't need him. That made her all the more desirable.

"Well," he continued, "I'm off today and tomorrow if you change your mind."

She put on her puffy jacket over her business suit and gave a silent wave as she exited into the garage. The only sound she heard was the garage door closing and the cats meowing at him to give them their snacks.

Chapter 35

"We are homing in on the subject," the director of the FBI said to Mac on the phone.

"Is it only one person?" Mac inquired. She assumed that this was a big operation due to the number of investigators involved.

"Just one guy," he said. "We are learning that his two partners died of natural causes years ago. This dude is old."

"Do you need me there?" Mac inquired.

"Yes, but I'm afraid that the WYDOT warning for the roads is pretty bad. I'm not sure it is safe to drive here."

"Burg wants to drive me," she responded, rolling her eyes to herself, but silently smirking at the same time.

"Good," he replied.

The Wyoming Department of Transportation, otherwise known as WYDOT was responsible for overseeing various aspects of transportation infrastructure and services in the state. It is in charge of the construction, maintenance, and repair of Wyoming's highways, bridges, and other roadways to ensure safe and efficient travel. It is also responsible for the issuance of driver's licenses, vehicle registrations, and titles, and for ensuring that drivers meet legal requirements to operate vehicles safely. It works closely with the Wyoming Highway Patrol to enforce road safety and respond to accidents and emergencies on state highways.

WYDOT also manages state airports and coordinates air travel regulations, safety, and infrastructure improvements related to aviation. In addition, it oversees rail transportation within the state and ensures the safety and efficiency of freight operations, which are critical to Wyoming's economy.

If WYDOT was issuing a state-wide warning about the safety of the highways that morning, Mac knew to pay attention. She called Burg and asked for a ride.

Chapter 36

When Charles Hoskinson heard helicopters overhead, he knew something was awry. His chocolate labs were whining at the commotion overhead. As he sauntered toward the barn with his two dogs at his heels, he saw that the horses were stir-crazy with the noise above.

However, he was wholly unprepared for the copter to land in his pasture away from the livestock that had long since scattered. This was a first for Hoskinson.

He froze in his tracks, not knowing what to do or expect.

He would quickly learn that in life, one must sometimes expect the unexpected.

Chapter 37

Mac and Burg drove slowly on Interstate 90 heading south from Sheridan to Buffalo, and then they would need to switch to smaller highways and local roads to reach Pumpkin Buttes, located in the central-eastern part of the state. Pumpkin Buttes are remote and located off main highways, so they would need to navigate through a combination of county roads after leaving the interstate.

Burg had a plow on the front of his truck and a winch in the event they encountered snow got stuck or needed to assist others. These items would come in handy that day.

Chapter 38

Burg drove his truck on the I-90 toward Casper as Mac read. The roads were not good. They were used to it, but Burg was pleased that she asked for help. She was fiercely independent and never asked for help. She would rather break her foot asking for help than the opposite, and he knew it. He finally felt like they were falling into place. He also knew that she was venturing into the dangerously hot water of prosecuting high-profile cases, and they both had discussed at length what this might look like.

They drove in silence but once they exited the interstate and headed south on Highway 59, and then east on dirt road 450, they were beyond cell reception. Burg had radio coverage and satellite coverage, and Stan was overhead in the helicopter for aerial guidance and safety. Mac had been too many times at risk and Burg was having none of it. He was going to protect the AG of the state of Wyoming, but most importantly to him. He was going to protect his wife who was pregnant for the first time, and his unborn son.

Chapter 39

Frank Morris woke up with a cough and a cold. He'd rarely missed a day of work in over 50 years, but his old bones were aching, and his body was tired. He felt terrible and his house was freezing cold.

He could have mustered the energy to at least drive to the Hoskinson ranch to report in, but he decided that he had earned the right not to do so.

As he lay in bed, cold and exhausted, he could hear helicopters overhead. He figured that the Game and Fish were chasing native wolves to scare them off from calves and sheep.

He was sorely wrong.

The Wyoming Game and Fish Department was responsible for managing and conserving wildlife, fish, and habitat. Its role was to oversee a variety of wildlife conservation, including hunting, fishing, and habitat restoration. The department also enforced state wildlife laws, issuance of licenses, and educational programs to the public. Its mission for wildlife conservation for current generations, while balancing the needs of humans and wildlife in Wyoming's ecosystems was of prime importance. The goal was to research while maintaining habitat improvement and initiatives to ensure sustainable populations of fish and wildlife.

The WGFD was not in helicopters overhead encircling Frank Morris's ranch. They were overhead because they were tailing Mac and Burg's SUV en route to his place.

Chapter 40

Burg had two daughters from a previous marriage and two grandchildren. He loved them dearly. He did not have a son, and his granddaughters did not carry his name.

Mac did not take his name in marriage. She had her identity and that was fine with both of them, but when she told him that she was pregnant, he was alarmed. She was 47 years old, and he was 61. He wasn't even thinking about having more kids, and she thought that the train had left the station.

When she went in for her four-month check-up and they asked her if she wanted to know the gender, she wasn't clued in enough to know that this was possible. She had been knee-deep in work and was supposed to read some books about what to expect, but she only read new laws on the illegal export of rare earth elements.

It didn't dawn on her that the rarest and most precious earth element was in her womb. And it was for Burg, a boy.

Chapter 41

Frank Morris was 92 and had lived 90 of those years by the time he was 30. He was fortunate enough to have escaped the Rock, and he knew his fortune was about to be called home to the Lord.

He was raised in the South by worshipers, and he never felt much religion until this day, but all of a sudden, he felt as if he was being called home. It was a strange and overwhelming feeling, yet comforting.

He heard a knock on his door, and he was too weak to answer. He heard the handle turn and the door open, and he felt a chilling wind enter his home.

He then heard a newly familiar voice. It was that of Charles Hoskinson.

"Are you okay?" Hoskinson asked.

Again, too weak to answer, he did not respond. Hoskinson made his way back to his bed.

"Are you ill?" Hoskinson inquired, his wife at his side holding a basket. The missus has made you some breakfast. She held up her neatly lined picnic basket and sat beside him. She poured him a tin of hot tea with honey and lemon and Hoskinson helped prop him to a point of consumption.

They spoon-fed him some nourishment while wrapping him in swaddling blankets and stoking a fire in his fireplace. His home was freezing cold, and they lay witness to a dying man.

Chapter 42

The experience of death for a dying person can vary widely depending on cultural, spiritual, and individual factors, as well as their state of consciousness. Some describe it as a peaceful release, a sense of letting go, or a gradual transition. Others might report visions of loved ones, bright lights, or feelings of warmth and comfort.

In near-death experiences, many people describe a tunnel of light, a feeling of detachment from their earthly body, or encountering a calming presence. For others, death may appear abstract – an overwhelming silence of darkness. There are also those who feel anxiety, fear, or confusion as the body and mind grapple with the unknown.

Ultimately, death, to a dying person, maybe a deeply subjective experience, shaped by personal beliefs, emotional state, and physiological responses.

For a criminal on death row, the approach of death can take on a distinct and complex psychological dimension, shaped by the awareness of an impending, scheduled end. Unlike those facing natural death, people on death row live with the knowledge of a specific time and method by which their lives will be taken, which can create intense feelings of dread, resignation, fear, or even defiance.

Some may come to terms with their fate, experiencing death as a final act of justice, closure, or atonement, especially if they have accepted responsibility for the, seeing death as the culmination of a long, traumatic, and often isolating process.

In the moments leading up to execution, death may seem like a sterile, procedural, and cold inevitability, often occurring in a clinical or prison environment, detached from the natural processes of life and death, their actions.

Some may experience emotional turmoil, grappling with thoughts of morality, redemption, or the afterlife. Others may detach emotionally, seeking solace in religious faith, meditation, or personal reflection. For many, the lead-up to death is likely to be one of intense psychological conflict with emotions ranging from fear and anxiety to numbness and acceptance.

The structured predetermined nature of execution on death row often strips away the natural unpredictability of death, leaving in its wake an environment of anticipation and the complex interplay of human emotions that accompany it.

Frank Morris, he had seen death row inmates of all types, and he was no stranger to their thoughts, emotions, fears or angst at this moment in time.

He felt the warmth of Charles Hoskinson and his dear wife on each side of him, and he truly felt loved for the first time in his life. It was okay to go to the light.

Chapter 43

Mac was not feeling well. The bumpy, winding dirt road was getting to her, and her morning sickness was still alive and well. Her doctor told her that morning sickness was a sign of a healthy baby. Mac thought that this was ironic and not funny.

Morning sickness was a common symptom of early pregnancy, typically characterized by nausea and, in some cases, vomiting. Despite its name, it could occur at any time of day. The intensity and duration could vary from woman to woman; for some, it was a mild inconvenience, while for others, it was severe and persistent, affecting daily life.

Morning sickness often begins around the sixth week of pregnancy and can last until the end of the first trimester, though it sometimes extends beyond that for some women. Hormonal changes, particularly rising levels of human chorionic gonadotropin and estrogen, are believed to trigger it. Other factors, such as heightened sensitivity to smells or an empty stomach, could exacerbate symptoms.

Whatever the case or duration, Mac was over it. She was tired of being tired and nauseous. She wasn't one to complain, but Burg could see it on her face. He pulled over.

"Fresh air," he asked.

She nodded and raced out of his vehicle to throw up. Once finished, he handed her his handkerchief, and she wiped her mouth.

"Better?" he asked.

She nodded. Then she pulled down her jeans to pee.

"This is what I have amounted to," she said. "Puking and peeing. Sexy talk."

"You are beautiful. Now get in the car."

Chapter 44

Hoskinson was confused about the helicopters until his cell phone rang. His phone was in Frank Morris's kitchen as he had left it there in order to carry a breakfast tray to his bedside. His wife nodded for him to answer despite the early hour, and he rose to do so.

"Yes," he said to the caller.

"Mr. Hoskinson, the is Sheriff Burgess of the Sheridan force, and my wife, I mean the County Prosecutor from Sheridan, is in the car with me and we are headed your way. We have spotty cell service, as you know, so if I lose you, I will call you back, but there are helicopters above you and above me tracking us."

"What in the bloody hell is going on?" Hoskinson asked.

"I will explain in person, but sit tight unless you feel that you are in danger."

"We are absolutely not in danger. We are sitting bedside to a dying man."

"Oh, I'm sorry, I did not know that he was dying. Quite frankly, we are surprised that he is alive," Burg said.

Hoskinson was confused and annoyed.

"Listen here, sheriff, this is my long-time friend and employee and ..." he was about to give Burg an earful when the line went dead. Cell service in Wyoming remains spotty, at best.

Chapter 45

Burg's number one deputy was tailing him, and she was given the order to serve Frank Morris with a search warrant. The warrant issued on the Hoskinson ranch only turned up with the legal export of uranium within and beyond the United States. His mining operations for other rare earth minerals also proved to be in line with all laws, rules, and regulations.

The Feds were convinced that the illegal export of uranium from Wyoming to Russia had been happening for decades and that it had recently ceased. That being the case, it would take months if not years to get Russia to cooperate with any negotiations regardless of sanctions. Therefore, the search for immediate, tangible evidence would need to be within the borders of Wyoming and any port used for trade. It would take time, but not years.

When Charles Hoskinson answered Frank Morris's door, he was about to deliver a scolding of a lifetime. Instead, he was met by Burg and Mac, who introduced themselves with pleasantries and had even stopped in Casper to bring chicken soup and electrolyte powers to add to beverages.

They explained what the issue was, and Hoskinson listened, as he had heard rumors in the uranium industry for years about illegal activity on the Pumpkin Buttes. He attributed to his competitors trying to trim the hedges on the complexities of the laws, and since he had always conducted business by the books, following all laws, he didn't pay it much mind.

Now his curiosity was peaked, and he was engaged in the art of listening, but all the while, feeling like this old man behind him could absolutely not have the wherewithal to pull off such a stunt. He was a dying man, after all.

Mac explained that she was the prosecutor on the case that went to trial earlier in the year and that she had grown to be educated in the intricacies of the uranium trade. She also explained that she had the benefit of the U.S. government's support in research, discovery, and experts who educated her in the prosecution of such crimes.

Hoskinson had calmed himself. But he did not believe that the old man dying in bed had anything to do with it.

Chapter 46

"Need the forensic dogs," Burg said to Mac. His conviction was identifiable, and she was unsure what to do with it.

"They are useless," Mac said.

He looked at her in three ways. Lawyer. Prosecutor. Wife. He knew he had made three mistakes.

Chapter 47

Guard dogs can serve as an effective deferent against intruders, but their ability to protect from illegal uranium harvesting is tenuous. Police dogs are primarily trained to detect substances such as drugs, explosives, firearms, and even human remains, using their highly developed sense of smell. However, detecting uranium specifically would be unlikely, as it doesn't have a distinctive odor like other materials dogs are trained to identify.

First, illegal uranium harvesting typically involved specialized equipment and personnel. If the individuals attempting to harvest uranium were well-organized and equipped, guard dogs might not be efficient to stop them. Detecting uranium or other radioactive materials requires tools such as Geiger counters or radiation detectors, rather than relying on scent. If law enforcement agencies were investigating the presence of uranium, they would typically use technology designed to detect radiation, rather than training dogs for this purpose.

Burg was good at forensics, but he did not understand the forensics of rare earth elements.

Uranium is often found in certain types of sedimentary rock, especially in regions known for past volcanic activity in Wyoming, sandstone formations are particularly known for uranium deposits.

Uranium can leach into groundwater, so testing water sources on a ranch such as Frank Morris's might help indicate nearby deposits.

The forensic team would need a Geiger counter to detect ionizing radiation in the form of gamma rays emitted by uranium and its decay products. Even more sensitive than Geiger counters, scintillation detectors can detect both alpha and beta particles along with gamma rays. In addition, portable spectrometers can identify the specific types of radioactive isotopes present, including uranium isotopes.

Airborne radiometric surveys in the form of planes or drones equipped with radiation detection equipment can cover large areas, scanning for anomalous levels of radiation indicative of uranium deposits.

Gamma-ray spectrometry is a technique that measures gamma radiation from uranium decay products like radon and thorium, providing detailed insights into uranium presence below the surface. Also, core drilling can be used if initial surveys suggest a high likelihood of uranium. This type of drilling might be performed to extract deep rock samples for laboratory analysis. This confirms the presence and concentration of uranium.

Chemical testing can confirm the concentration of uranium in soil, rock, or water samples by analyzing the chemical composition.

Wyoming is home to some of the largest uranium reserves in the U.S., with many deposits found in sandstone formations, especially in areas like the Powder River Basin where Pumpkin Buttes is located as well as the Hoskinson ranch and Frank Morris's ranch. In the past, Wyoming was a major center for uranium mining, and many ranches in this general region with known uranium-bearing formations still exist.

Mac and Burg, in conjunction with the feds, would need to engage a similar team that Mac had just utilized in prosecuting the two defendants convicted of illegal export of uranium from Wyoming to Russia. They would need to re-engage the geologists and other professionals to survey the Frank Morris ranch to determine if there was uranium on his ranch, which was highly likely, but more importantly, if it had been mined and if so, what happened to it.

This was the mission.

Chapter 48

Charles Hoskinson and his wife were sitting bedside around the clock taking care of Frank Morris. It was nearly impossible for him to get comfortable, as the cancer had spread to his bones, and he was in agony. Not to mention the commotion of noise from the uranium forensic team scanning all sources of uranium extraction on his ranch. The feds had swooped in with the forensic teams and they were fast confirming what was expected to have happened.

It wasn't long before it was confirmed that not only had uranium been extracted from the Morris ranch, but also neodymium, praseodymium, and scandium. These four rare earth elements used in high tech industries captured big money on the up-and-up, let alone what they captured on the black market.

The black market for rare earth elements such as neodymium, praseodymium, and scandium and radioactive matters like uranium is an extremely secretive illegal trade, and it would be difficult for Mac to provide a jury with exact figures on Frank Morris was charged with the crime of illegal export of these elements. However, the demand and price for these elements can vary based on several factors, such as purity, quantity, and their intended use.

Uranium the legal market, uranium oxide ("yellowcake") sells for about $50-70 per pound, but this can vary with geopolitical facts and supply-demand. On the black market, prices are much harder to estimate, and any trade is illegal highly dangerous, and subject to strict international controls.

Prices can vary significantly, but reports suggest black market deals could fetch up to $5,000 - $10,000 per kilogram depending on the purity and enrichment level (whether it is raw uranium or enriched).

Selling uranium illegally attracts severe penalties due to its potential use in weapons or dirty bombs.

Neodymium is legally value around $100-$150 per kilogram. It's a crucial element in the production of powerful magnets used in electronics and clean energy technology. On the black market, neodymium might be sold at inflated prices due to limited access to legitimate sources, possibly fetching $200-$500 per kilogram in illegal markets where high-tech industries may struggle to obtain it.

Praseodymium, used similarly to neodymium in high-strength magnets and some alloys, has a legal market value of $70-$100 per kilogram. Like neodymium, praseodymium on the black market could command higher prices, potentially $200-$400 per kilogram for illegal buyers needing the element for industrial applications.

Scandium is much rarer and expensive, with legal market prices ranging from $3,000 to $5,000 per kilogram due to its limited supply and use in aerospace components and high-performance alloys. On the black market, scandium could command even higher prices, possibly $5,000-$10,000 per kilogram depending on the demand from industries unable to secure legitimate supplies.

The black market for these elements operates in the shadows, and prices are highly speculative. For uranium, the trade is tightly controlled and extremely risky due to its radioactive properties and potential for weaponization.

For rare earth elements like neodymium, praseodymium, and scandium, while less dangerous, illegal trade would likely involve inflated prices due to restricted access, especially for high-tech and industrial uses.

For Mac, she could prove up her case to a jury even with speculative numbers. The crime was the crime, and the feds would back her charging Frank Morris with the illegal export of all four rare earth elements.

Time was of the essence, as Frank Morris was a dying man, and getting a case to trial for a man on his deathbed was a hard sell. However, when the U.S. government was pushing hard for this to happen during Frank Morris's lifetime, things were moving quickly and Judge Maurita Redle was finding out that she had better be expedient with the handling of the recently filed criminal charges against Frank Morris for the illegal export to Russia of uranium, neodymium, praseodymium and scandium.

These charges were seminal in Wyoming and no case had to date been prosecuted for the three rare earth elements. Mac had recently proven her case for the illegal export of uranium from Wyoming to Russia. This new case before Judge Maurita Redle was garnering the attention of media from around the world. Set in the quintessential small western town of Sheridan, Wyoming.

Chapter 49

Charles Hoskinson did not have any part in allowing Burg's men to escort Frank Morris to jail pending trial. He hired private lawyers to ban such activity, citing numerous other cases in the U.S. of elderly charged criminals and their ability to have their presence in court waived.

Judge Maurita Redle was inclined to agree and not require this dying old man's presence in court. She didn't want him dying on her watch. No one was precisely sure of his exact age, but suffice it to say, he was somewhere in his 90's. And he had cancer in his bones and now his brain and what they would soon discover, in his spinal fluid. This was tantamount to death within days or weeks at the most.

When cancer spreads to the spinal fluid, this condition is known as leptomeningeal disease (LMD) or leptomeningeal carcinomatosis. It is a serious complication, indicating that the cancer has metastasized to the meninges (the membranes surrounding the brain and spinal cord) and the cerebrospinal fluid. This condition is often associated with a poor prognosis, and life expectancy can be significantly reduced.

The factors affecting the prognosis include the type of cancer, the extent of the disease, and treatment options Breast and lung cancer typically have a somewhat longer survival rate compared to other cancers. Melanoma has a more aggressive course once it spreads to the spinal fluid. Hematologic cancers such as leukemia and lymphoma can sometimes respond to aggressive treatment, improving survival rates slightly.

The extent to the disease and how far it has spread within the central nervous system can influence prognosis. Treatment options regardless of the type of cancer and the spread thereof involves administering chemotherapy directly into the spinal fluid to target cancer cells more effectively. Radiation can help alleviate symptoms and prolong life in select cases. Palliative care focuses on improving the quality of life, as curative treatments are usually not effective.

Life expectancy for individuals like Frank Morris who has lung cancer that has metastasized is short. The survival rate on average may be four to six weeks without treatment, and three to six months with treatment. For Frank, there were no treatment options and, therefore, one could expect him to live most likely not more than one month.

The trial would not be finished within one month and, therefore, Judge Redle knew that the best option would be for Frank Morris to stipulate to a plea deal wherein he pleaded guilty to all charges, with any resulting sentence to be served at his home on the ranch until his certain death. That was her recommendation to Mac, the feds, and all lawyers, whether publicly engaged or privately engaged. And all parties involved knew that this would be how it was going to ultimately play out.

They agreed to allow any plea deal reached to be from a WebEx video into Judge Redle's courtroom with all players present. But the audience was not prepared to learn what Frank Morris would tell him from his deathbed.

Chapter 50

"All rise," the bailiff announced as Judge Maurita Redl walked into the courtroom in her black robe. She took the bench and when she was seated, the rest of the gallery sat. The large television screen to Judge Redle's left in the corner of her courtroom came to life and as her clerk fiddled with some settings on the computer, the screen focused on an old man in his bed in night clothes, pale, thin, and wrinkled. Charle Hoskinson sat at his side, along with two private lawyers that Hoskinson had engaged to represent Frank Morris.

"Do we have a plea deal to enter into this morning?" Judge Redle inquired.

"We do, your Honor," Mac said while standing at the prosecutor's desk. "We have negotiated this deal in good faith with the defendant and his attorneys."

"First of all, your Honor, my name is not Larry Cook. My legal name is Frank Morris. I assumed the identity of Larry Cook sometime around 1965 and no one has questioned me about my name in these parts. But the truth is that I am the Frank Morris who escaped Alcatraz in 1962 along with the Anglin brothers. We did survive the swim, and we promptly headed East, and we looked for somewhere remote to live," Frank started.

There was an audible gasp in the courtroom. Mac was in utter shock. She had no idea that Larry Cook was not Larry Cook.

He had been employed on the Hoskinson ranch for so long that no one questioned his identity, including Mac. Even Charles Hoskinson had just learned this information.

Judge Redle struck her gavel and said, "Order in my courtroom.: She turned her attention to Frank Morris. "Larry Cook also known as Frank Morris, the charges pending remain the same regardless of your name. I need you to understand this before we proceed."

"Yes, your Honor, I understand."

"You may continue with your plea," Judge Redle said.

"I have been living in these parts since we escaped. We had to assume new identities, as you would understand, as we were the most wanted men in the country for decades."

"I understand. Please proceed and let the record reflect that all pending charges will be augmented to include any and all aliases you have ever used," Mac interjected from the prosecutor's table. She was wearing her navy suit and a cream blouse, and her long, auburn hair was pulled back in a professional French twist.

"I admit that the Anglin brothers and I illegally exported uranium, neodymium, praseodymium, and scandium from my ranch and the Hoskinson ranch for many years. We are guilty of selling these items on the black market to Russia dating back to the 1980s. The only reason that I stopped was because both Anglin brothers died years back from the same lung cancer that plagues me now."

His voice was cracking. Charles Hoskinson propped him up more in his bed and offered him a sip of water.

"So, you admit to all pending charges in exchange for a life sentence and a disgorgement of profits, is that correct?" Mac asked.

"Yes, it is," Morris said.

"You understand that this Court will assign you to house arrest until death, correct?" Mac confirmed.

"Yes, I understand. I am in hospice, and it is not expected that I live more than a few weeks. I will sign over all bank accounts and the deed to my ranch in exchange for this sentence," Morris continued.

It was obvious that he was growing weary. His coloring was fading, as was the strength of his voice.

"The Court accepts your plea, and you are hereby sentenced to life without the possibility of parole and a discouragement of all profits," Judge Redle pronounced.

Frank Morris nodded in a reflection of his pending doom. He was a dying man, and he was lucky that he was able to live half of his life as a free man and he knew it. His sense of conviction regarding this fact was not lost on him.

"Thank you for saving the State of Wyoming and the United States government from the time and expense of a trial," Judge Redle said. "Godspeed to you." She felt tears welling in her eyes. She had never issued what was essentially a death sentence before.

"Thank you, your Honor," Morris mustered.

"We are going to sign out," Hoskinson interjected. I am afraid that this old man is not long for this world, and it is time for his morphine."

"Understood," Mac said. "We can only wish you a sense of peace." She, too, was emotional about this plea. She did not see his true identity coming and she was in shock.

Chapter 51

The media had a field day with this breaking news about the true identity of Frank Morris and that the last surviving member of the three men who escaped The Rock in 1962 had just exposed his true identity while pleading guilty to the illegal export of rare earth elements in the Pumpkin Buttes of Wyoming.

This would go down in history as one of the most shocking discoveries in the history of the courtrooms of the world.

###

9 79833 0481224